THE JUNIOR NOVELIZATION

BALTO

THE JUNIOR NOVELIZATION

Adapted by Cindy Chang

Based on the motion picture story by Cliff Ruby & Elana Lesser

Screenplay by Cliff Ruby & Elana Lesser and
Roger Schulman & David Cohen

Hippo
HOLLYWOOD

Scholastic Children's Books,
Commonwealth House, 1-19 New Oxford Street,
London WC1A 1NU, UK
a division of Scholastic Ltd
London~New York~Toronto~Sydney~Auckland

First published in the US by Grosset & Dunlap, Inc., 1995. A member of The
Putnam & Grosset Group, New York. GROSSET & DUNLAP is a trademark
of Grosset & Dunlap, Inc. Published simultaneously in Canada.
First published in the UK by Scholastic Ltd, 1996

ISBN 0 590 13953 3

Printed by Cox & Wyman Ltd, Reading, Berks.

10 9 8 7 6 5 4 3 2 1

CHAPTER 1

1925
Nome, Alaska

W*hoosh!* A powerful purebred silver-and-charcoal malamute led a dog sled team down a snow-covered trail. His steel-blue eyes looked steadily out of the mask on his face. Sunlight gleamed off his golden championship collar.

"Steele! We're not going to make it!" yelled Star, a nervous gray-and-cream husky, as they approached a narrow pass.

But Steele kept up his pace. He closed in on a small husky leading another, less experienced team, bared his fangs, and growled. That was all it took to send the other team careening out of control. As the musher and dogs were thrown off the trail, Steele flashed a satisfied smile and pulled his own team through the pass—victorious!

The fallen musher shook his fist furiously. "Ha!"

Steele scoffed as he raced on toward Nome and the finish line. Down the trail, a spotter on the ravine caught sight of Steele's team. He pointed his flare pistol skyward and pulled the trigger. *Bumpf!*

"It's the three-mile marker!" Balto shouted when he saw the flare explode. "We're going to miss the end of the race!"

On the edge of the small town of Nome, Balto, a cheerful, gray half-husky, half-wolf, balanced precariously on the top of a fence and tried to hoist up his friend Boris, a cranky Russian snow goose.

"You think I care about a bunch of crazy dogs all trying to outrun each other in the freezing cold?" Boris asked. "Like there was only one tree in all of Alaska!"

Balto just ignored the goose's comment. "Let's go, Boris!" he barked. "We can cut through town!"

Boris shook his head. "Oh, no! I am country bird. I stay out of there!"

But Balto was already off. He hopped onto the rooftop of a building lining Front Street and raced toward the center of town.

Boris struggled to keep up. "Every time there is a race, you run around like you're in it!"

"Maybe one day I will be!" Balto called cheerfully over his shoulder.

Then—*Bumpf!*—another flare exploded in the sky.

"It's the two-mile mark! Come on, Boris. We don't want to miss the finish!"

"Oh! That would be a tragedy!" Boris said sarcastically.

As Balto ran by the carpenter's shop, a young girl's voice made him stop. He propped his paws on the windowsill and peered in. There was Rosy, an eight-year-old with twinkling blue eyes and a cheerful smile. She laughed as a child-sized dog sled was handed to her. Beside her, a pretty rust-and-cream husky named Jenna looked on.

Balto sighed. He could have watched Jenna all day long. She was definitely the prettiest dog in Nome. But then Balto remembered the race. With one last glance, he hopped down from the windowsill and headed on toward the finish line, leaving Rosy and Jenna to enjoy their present.

"I love these runners! I love this sled!" Rosy cried as she hitched Jenna to the sled. "Jenna, you're lead dog! Mush!"

Jenna's bright bandanna shook gracefully as she happily barked back.

"Well, if you're going to drive a dog sled," Rosy's mother told her, "then you'll need this." She plopped a small furry musher's hat on Rosy's head. It fell forward, covering her eyes. But Rosy didn't care.

"A real musher's hat! We're a real sled team now!

Thank you! Thank you! Thank you!" Rosy told her parents and the carpenter. Then she hopped onto the sled. "Jenna! Come on, girl! Mush!" And Rosy and Jenna mushed out the door.

The whole length of Front Street was crowded with people and dogs. Despite the freezing cold and the falling snow, the entire town had turned out to watch the first race of the season. Rosy squeezed herself in among the other spectators, and Jenna trotted over to her friends Sylvie, an elegant Afghan, and Dixie, a snowy, showy malamute.

Dixie pretended to gaze into the sky as she tried to show off a brand-new sparkling collar. "Good morning, Jenna. Should be a close race, don't you think?" Dixie said, throwing her head back even more. "Maybe even *neck and neck.*"

Jenna didn't get Dixie's point right away.

"Say something about her new collar." Sylvie nudged her. "Before she gets whiplash."

"Ooooh!" Jenna nodded. "Um, Dixie, what a pretty collar. Is it new?"

"What, *this* old thing?" Dixie squealed. "Yes! Do you think Steele will notice?"

"I'm afraid the only way Steele notices anyone is if they're wearing a mirror," Jenna remarked. Steele was one dog she could live without.

Just then someone shouted, "They're coming!" And the dogs' attention turned back to the race.

Across the street, Balto had found his own spot—with a perfect view of the finish line *and* Jenna. Balto had had a crush on Jenna from the first moment he saw her. He wished he had the courage to go over and start talking to her. But he just couldn't. Everyone in town thought he was wild—just because he was half-wolf. What if Jenna did too? But there was no time to worry about that now. The sleds were getting closer, and Steele was in the lead.

From her own spectator spot, Rosy waved her new hat to welcome the team in. "Come on, Steele!" she shouted. Then suddenly a gust of wind blew up and swept the furry hat out of Rosy's hand—and right into the path of the oncoming team!

"My hat!" Rosy shouted. Rosy and Jenna looked at the furry bundle—and at the team bearing down on it—in horror.

Balto glanced back and forth between Steele and the hat. In seconds, the hat was going to be crushed—unless . . . Without a second thought, Balto raced out into the street. Steele was only yards away—and rapidly approaching!

"It's that wild dog!" someone on the sidelines shouted.

"He's trying to ruin the race!"

Suddenly everyone was shouting at Balto, and

Steele was barking at him too. "Out of my way, *lobo!*" he barked.

Boris cringed on the sidelines, waiting for the impact . . . but it never happened.

Balto paced Steele for a few seconds, as Steele bared his fangs and lunged angrily at him. Of course, all Balto cared about was getting Rosy's hat. He cut easily in front of Steele and plucked the hat from the snowy street.

Whoosh! Steele's team rushed by, missing Balto by inches. With a little shake, Balto gave a relieved sigh and jogged to the other side of the street with the hat.

Steele's sled crossed the finish line to a cheering crowd. Nikki, a plump, cocky husky, called out to Steele from down the line. "Congratulations there, boss. It was a pleasure running behind you! Of course, the *view* got monotonous."

But Steele didn't pay any attention to him. He had spotted something more interesting—Jenna! Haughtily, he slipped out of his harness and strutted over to the dogs. Steele had a weakness for redheads, and he'd had his eye on Jenna for a long time. Jenna never seemed half as interested in him, but Steele was sure she would succumb to his charms sooner or later. After all, didn't everyone?

Meanwhile, Balto was already across the street, offering the hat to Rosy.

"Balto! What a crazy thing to do!" Rosy exclaimed

with a big smile. Then she glanced at Jenna. "And just to show off to a pretty girl!"

Embarrassed, Jenna quickly turned away. But Rosy just laughed and gave Balto a hug. "I'm sure Jenna would love to have you on our team!"

Then suddenly, a hand pulled Rosy away. "Rosy! Stay away from that dog! He might bite you. He's half-wolf." It was Rosy's father.

Balto's smile faded, and he shrank back with his head down. Sadly Balto began to walk away.

Rosy frowned and looked up at her father. "Now you've hurt his feelings!" she said.

But her father was already looking at Steele. "Good race, Steele!" he said as the dog walked over.

Steele strutted past and headed straight for Jenna. Dixie's tail wagged excitedly. "Felicitations and congratulations, Steele!" she gushed as he approached.

"Ladies." Steele nodded politely to Sylvie and Dixie, but it was clear he had eyes only for Jenna. He greeted her in a boastful voice. "Hi there, Jenna! Enjoy the race?"

"Yeah, almost as much as you did," Jenna said.

Steele took her comment—like he took everything—as a compliment. "Thanks!" He grinned. Then he inched closer. "Hey, Jenna, let's go celebrate. I know where all the bones are buried."

"Sorry, Steele. Suddenly I've lost my appetite."

Steele's grin quickly disappeared. "Oh, maybe your

taste runs more toward wolf," he said nastily, nodding toward Balto.

But before Jenna could reply, Rosy's cheerful voice called to her. "Jenna! Come on, girl."

"Sorry, Steele," said Jenna. "My girl is calling me."

After the race, Boris tried, without much success, to comfort Balto. But as they walked along the empty alley behind Front Street, Balto's ears perked up. Was that Rosy? Balto followed the voice around the corner—and came nose-to-nose with Jenna! Balto swallowed hard. Here was his chance to talk to her! But, of course, Balto couldn't think of a single thing to say.

"Jenna! Come on!" Rosy's high, sweet voice floated over to them.

Jenna turned to see Rosy walking toward her, and by the time she turned back, Balto was gone. *Too bad*, thought Jenna. She didn't know Balto very well, but she liked him, no matter what the others said. She could tell he was gentle and kind, not wild. She looked down at the big paw prints trailing away in the snow. *Maybe next time*, she thought.

Meanwhile, Balto and Boris were almost out of town. Then suddenly, Steele and his gang of dogs sauntered up behind them.

"Didn't make the team, *Bingo?*" Steele teased. His dog buddies doubled over, laughing.

"Don't listen to him. Don't look at him," Boris warned Balto. "Live a long life."

But Steele's bullying was too much for Balto to take. He whipped around and faced Steele. "My name's *Balto!*" he said.

"But you can call him idiot," mumbled Boris.

"I'm sorry *Balto*. *Balto* the half-breed," mocked Steele. Then he turned to Boris. "Hey, old goose, you a half-breed too, huh? Part turkey? Gobble, gobble, gobble." Steele's dogs, Star, Nikki, and a dim-witted husky named Kaltag, joined in the taunting.

"Just leave him out of this, Steele," Balto said. He moved to stand between Boris and Steele.

But Steele didn't care. Boris wasn't the one he was after. "Oh, Balto," he said, "I've got a message for your mother . . . *A-whooo!*" Steele howled like a wolf. "Hi, Mom!" He laughed.

Balto had had enough. His eyes closed into slits and a growl rumbled up from deep inside his throat. Steele's dogs stopped laughing, one by one.

"Get him!" Steele ordered.

Boris cringed and jumped back as Steele's dogs started barking wildly. But Balto held his ground.

Steele's voice rose above the uproar. "Get out of here, wolf dog! Get back to your pack!"

"Maybe it's the fear talking, but I am seeing wisdom in this advice," said Boris. "Maybe we go now, huh, Balto? Now!"

Balto stared at Steele, but finally backed down. He knew Boris was right. A fight would not solve anything. And so, without another word, Balto turned and walked away.

CHAPTER 2

The setting sun colored the sky a deep orange as Balto and Boris walked across the snow-covered tundra toward the small harbor just outside of town.

Along the harbor, old, abandoned fishing boats dotted the coast. The biggest, a gold dredger, was the official meeting place for all the dogs of Nome. And just beyond that was Balto and Boris's home—an old wooden trawler.

As soon as Balto and Boris were inside, Balto crawled under his rug, tired and saddened from the hard day. Boris tried as best he could to cheer Balto up. He offered bones, toys, even did a little dance, but Balto just burrowed deeper under his rug.

Then suddenly, Balto lifted his head. A giant V of geese flew by, honking overhead. Boris looked up too.

"Homesick, Boris?" Balto asked. "Ever think about going back?"

"Naw," said Boris. "I'm sticking here until I'm sure you can stand on your own four feet."

"*You're* taking care of *me*?" Balto asked, smiling.

"Do not thank me," Boris replied.

Then Balto caught a whiff of a scent that made his nose wrinkle. "I smell herring."

Boris looked up. "The herring are flying south too?"

Balto shook his head. "Must be Muk and Luk," he said.

"Oh, great!" groaned Boris. Then he heard a voice from outside. "Uncle Borrrrriiiiiisssss!"

"Oh, no!" Boris cringed. And suddenly two roly-poly polar bear cubs came barreling toward him. "No hugging! No licking!" Boris shouted just as Luk, the younger but larger of the two, threw his arms around the goose and licked him lovingly.

"Luk says he's glad to see you!" said Muk. "He loves you, Uncle Boris."

Luk finally let go of Boris, who angrily stomped off. Luk looked over at Muk and made a few questioning grunts.

"Of course he's glad to see us," Muk replied. "He loves us! Don't you, Uncle Boris?"

Boris walked to the door, calling out to the cubs, "Sure, sure, boychicks. Now, we play a game."

"Yes please, Uncle Boris!" said Muk. Luk nodded eagerly.

"Ready? Race you to the shore! One, two, three, go!" Boris yelled.

Muk and Luk raced away, giggling.

"They win!" Boris shouted as the cubs disappeared behind a mound of snow. Then suddenly the giggling turned into shrieks. "Help! We can't swim! We're drowning! Save us!"

Balto and Boris sprinted toward the mound of snow. They climbed the small ridge and rolled their eyes at what they saw below—the two cubs flailing in a puddle of icy water. Their creamy fur was barely wet.

"Bears! Fellas! Idiot balls of fluff!" Boris yelled down to Muk and Luk.

"Easy, Boris. You know how sensitive they are," Balto said. "Muk! Luk!" he called. "Look! You're all right! You're *not drowning!*"

"He has point, bears," Boris said, more patiently this time. "You are not drowning because, if you will pause one moment you will observe perhaps, *tide is out!*" Boris screamed the last few words.

The bears stopped thrashing and slowly opened their eyes. They looked down at the inch of water they were sitting in, then at each other. Muk shook his head and looked ashamed. Luk, who still had not mastered the art of speech, gave a sad little sigh.

"He said *what?*" Boris asked, looking to Muk for the translation.

The little bear cleared his throat. " 'Oh, the shame of the polar bear who fears the water. No wonder we are shunned by our fellow bears. Woe is us,' is what

he said . . . kind of pathetic, really," Muk explained.

"What, more whimpering?" Boris groaned. "Between you and Balto, is like sad Russian novel around here! *Lighten up!*" And with a flap of his wings, Boris led everyone inside.

For the rest of the evening, Balto sat around, staring into space and sighing.

"And what is so interesting?" Boris asked, trying to see what Balto was staring at.

"Jenna," Balto sighed with a dreamy expression.

"Is love," cooed Boris. "So go make move!"

"Nah. She's not my type." Balto shook his head. *I'm not her type, is more like it*, he thought to himself. "Really," he told Boris.

But Boris knew Balto too well. "And why not?" he argued. "This wolf business again? What is wrong with being half-half, I'd like to know? Sometimes I wish like crazy I was half eagle!" Boris said.

"Why?" asked Balto.

"Better profile, for one thing," Boris stated firmly. "No one eats you, for another."

Balto chuckled, but his mind wasn't changed. It was no use. Jenna would never be interested in him.

CHAPTER 3

Jenna paced in front of the large house that served as Nome's hospital. Rosy and her parents had been inside for only an hour, but Jenna felt as if she'd been waiting forever. Every now and then she caught a glimpse of Rosy through a window, but not for very long.

For the past several days, Jenna had noticed that Rosy had not been feeling well. She couldn't run or play as much as usual. Finally, Rosy's parents had taken her to see the doctor. Jenna hadn't been too worried at first, but now she was starting to get more and more concerned.

"Jenna! Jenna! Hi, girl!" Suddenly Rosy came out the front door. She reached for Jenna and stroked her ears. Jenna barked happily, then ran off expecting Rosy to join her.

Rosy laughed and started to chase Jenna, but she quickly stumbled to a stop, coughing uncontrollably. Worried, Jenna hurried back to Rosy's side. She had never seen Rosy so sick before.

"Rosy! Come on, honey. The doctor's waiting,"

Rosy's father called out from the doorway.

Reluctantly, Rosy obeyed. She was still coughing as her father led her back inside.

Jenna went back to pacing and waiting for Rosy to come back out. Impatient, Jenna made her way around to the side of the building, where she spied a lit window. She balanced on a bench and peeked inside.

Light from the room shone on Jenna's worried face. The room was full of sick children. Some were coughing; others were sleeping. Jenna shuddered, but she was happy to see that Rosy was not in there.

Jenna walked along the bench to the next window. She propped her paws up on the windowsill and looked inside. There was Rosy. The doctor was examining her throat. As Rosy's parents looked on anxiously, the doctor frowned and rubbed his beard.

Jenna was so caught up in watching Rosy, she didn't even notice Balto walking by. But he noticed her. Suddenly full of confidence, Balto came up behind Jenna.

"Jenna?" he said, his voice breaking slightly.

Jenna glanced over her shoulder. "Balto. Uh, hi," she said, distracted. Then she turned back to the window.

But Balto kept up the conversation. "Hi . . . look . . . it's just a shot in the dark, but I was wondering if . . . I don't know, maybe you'd like to go chase a few-

sticksbymoonlight." The last few words rushed out. Then Balto caught his breath and waited for her reply.

But Jenna just kept looking in the window. She didn't say a word. She didn't even turn around.

Balto's shoulders slumped and his hope-filled smile faded. He should have known she would never be interested in him.

Balto turned and started to walk away, then something stopped him. He looked back at Jenna and realized what it was. She was crying. "Jenna? What's wrong?" he asked gently.

"Rosy's in there," Jenna sobbed.

Balto inched closer. "In the hospital? Why?"

"She feels warm. She has a terrible cough," Jenna explained.

Balto hopped onto the bench and looked in the window, too. No one in the room was smiling. "They all look so worried," he said.

"Balto, what's wrong with her?" Jenna cried.

Balto shook his head. "I'm not sure. But I know how to find out." He jumped off the bench. "Come on."

Balto led Jenna to a woodshed at the back of the hospital. "After you," he said politely, and gestured for Jenna to enter.

Balto reached over Jenna's head to wipe away cobwebs that crisscrossed the doorway. As he pulled back his front leg, he caught Jenna staring at his paws.

"Balto!"

"Big feet kind of run in my family," Balto explained with an embarrassed smile. "At least, one side of my family."

The shed, dimly lit by a boiler in the corner, led down to a narrow crawl space just below the hospital floor. "Stay close," Balto instructed as they inched along the dark space, side by side.

"No problem there," Jenna replied. "It's so gloomy down here. Not that I'm scared or anything!"

Balto tried to reassure her. "Gloomy? Are you kidding? This is the most beautiful spot in the world. Dogs travel for years just to be right here," he joked.

"Here? I can't see why," Jenna replied, confused.

"That's because you're looking at the bowl half empty," Balto said. He grouped some pieces of broken glass together with his nose. "See this? It's the polar ice caps."

"Balto, those are broken bottles. And they're not half empty—they're *all* empty!" Jenna said.

Balto smiled and nodded toward a shaft of light spilling through a ventilation grate. "The sun," he said.

"Huh?" Jenna replied.

Balto rearranged the glass again to capture the light perfectly. Suddenly the tiny crawl space exploded into a rainbow of colors.

Jenna gasped, enchanted by the dancing lights.

"The Aurora Borealis!" she cried, excitedly. "Balto, you're right! It's beautiful!"

"Yes, beautiful," Balto agreed. But he was not looking at the lights. He was looking at Jenna.

Just then, Jenna and Balto heard footsteps directly above them. They both looked up and heard the authoritative voice of the doctor. "Good night, Rosy."

Quickly, the dogs moved to a spot directly underneath the voice.

"I'm so cold," they heard Rosy say weakly, between coughs.

"Well, I have another blanket right here," the doctor told her. "Now you stay warm and get some rest."

Then the doctor and Rosy's father went into another room. Down below, the dogs scrambled to keep up with the men.

"Doctor, how is she?" Rosy's father asked.

The doctor waited a moment to reply. "Exhausted from coughing. Her fever's getting worse. Looks like diphtheria—she's the eighteenth case this week." He sighed. "And I'm out of antitoxin."

Jenna didn't know exactly what the doctor meant, but she knew it wasn't good. She raced out of the crawl space. She wanted to be with Rosy.

Balto chased after her. "Jenna! Jenna! I'm sorry! I didn't mean to upset you. I shouldn't have brought you here!"

Jenna stopped, and Balto caught up with her in the woodshed.

"No. I'm glad you did," Jenna murmured, ashamed of herself for running off like that.

Suddenly a shadowy figure appeared in the dark alley outside. A string of sausages dangled from its mouth. Slowly it moved into the light.

"Steele!" Jenna gasped.

Balto's heart sank. *Why Steele? Why now?*

"Well, well. What's wrong with *this* picture? Join me for dinner, Jenna?" Steele tossed his head, causing the sausage string to dance. "You start at one end, I'll start at the other. And when we get to the middle . . . well, *you* tell me." Steele flashed a fang-filled smile.

"All right, Steele." Balto began to move into the alley. He wasn't going to be humiliated in front of Jenna.

"No, Balto." Jenna stopped Balto and gave him a wink. She knew how to handle Steele. Coyly she moved in closer to the bully. "Gee, Steele," she said softly, "I have to admit, your offer is very tempting."

"It is!" Steele said confidently.

"But these days," Jenna said, smiling, "I prefer my meat cooked."

All of a sudden, Steele's smug grin turned into a grimace. "OW!" he cried. Jenna had backed him into the boiler! Steele howled in pain, dropping the sausages.

"What's all the noise?" Suddenly, across the alley, the butcher opened the back door of his shop, and Rosy's father came out of the hospital. Steele froze, then picked up the sausages and tossed them over near Balto's feet.

"Looks like Balto found his way into the meat locker," Rosy's father said, assuming that Balto had stolen the food.

"It's a good thing Steele was here!" replied the butcher. He threw the sausages to Steele. "Good boy, Steele! You've earned these. Besides, I can't do anything with them after that wild animal touched them!" Then he turned toward Balto. "Go on!" he bellowed. "Get out of here, thief!" He shook his fist as Balto fled.

While Steele wagged his tail innocently, Jenna started to run after Balto. But Rosy's father grabbed her bandanna. "Come on, Jenna. Let's go home," he said.

As he pulled her toward the door, Jenna turned to look for Balto. But all she could see was a set of large tracks leading out of the alley.

CHAPTER 4

By early the next morning, the hospital was quarantined and the doctor was dictating a telegram to Anchorage:

ANCHORAGE. STOP.
REPEAT URGENT REQUEST. STOP.
MORE DIPHTHERIA ANTITOXIN. STOP.
NOME IN GRAVE DANGER. STOP.
PLEASE HELP. STOP.

The first response was not good news:

NOME. STOP.
BAY FROZEN OVER. STOP.
CANNOT SHIP ANTITOXIN BY SEA. STOP.
WILL TRY BY AIR. STOP.

The next reply was even worse:

NOME. STOP.
STORM AT AIRPORT. STOP.
PLANES GROUNDED UNTIL STORM CLEARS. STOP.
MANY REGRETS. STOP.

Finally a telegram came in from Juneau, the state capital:

FROM JUNEAU. OFFICE OF GOVERNOR. STOP.

SHIPPING ANTITOXIN BY RAIL. STOP.

TRAIN LINE ENDS AT NENANA. STOP.

SELECT FASTEST DOGS TO MEET TRAIN. STOP.

SLED TEAM TO CARRY ANTITOXIN FROM NENANA TO
  NOME. STOP.

GOD WILLING TRAIN WILL MAKE IT THROUGH. STOP.

AND SO WILL DOGS. STOP.

The next morning, people and dogs alike gathered along Front Street. The crowd was excited but quiet. This was serious business. They were picking a dog team to go to Nenana to bring back the antitoxin. It was the only way to save the sick children.

Dogs waited restlessly along the starting line, while mushers milled around. Steele looked over the running dogs with contempt. He didn't have to run this race—he knew he would be leading the team of the fastest dogs.

"Just look at Steele! He's going to save the entire town. He's positively mag-nesium!" Dixie sighed.

"It's not exactly a one-dog show, Dixie. They're racing to see who's going to be on the dog sled *team*," Jenna stressed, nodding her head toward the other dogs.

"What's with you, Jenna? Steele's a genuine hero, but do you give him a sniff?" Dixie remarked.

"That's because Jenna is running with Balto," Sylvie said.

"No! Do tell!" Dixie squealed. Her eyes opened wide and her ears perked up.

Sylvie went on. "She was seen in the boiler room the other night with Balto, and they went in together and they left together and I heard it all from a very reliable source and don't bother to deny it." Sylvie looked at Jenna.

Jenna smiled, then cleared her throat. "Well, then, I won't."

"I'm speechless!" Dixie declared, shocked.

▼▼▼

Balto, meanwhile, was pacing nervously near the edge of town.

"Balto, racing is a spectator sport. It requires very little preparation. You sit, you arrange refreshments," Boris told him.

"I'm not watching the race, I'm running it," Balto announced.

"You said what?" Boris sputtered.

"Hey, look. I want to help Rosy get better. I can get that medicine through," Balto replied.

"First of all, get it through your head that they wouldn't put you on a sled team even if you *did* win," Boris said flatly.

Balto sighed. "Boris, did you ever think maybe

you're the reason the other geese fly south?"

But Boris waved him off. "If only your feet were as fast as your mouth!"

Suddenly they heard the announcer calling dogs to the starting line. Balto's ears perked up. "They're starting. Wish me luck!" he called as he trotted off.

"Luck! I don't wish you luck! I wish you sense!" Boris called back. But under his breath, he said, "Good luck, kiddo!" Boris knew Balto could do it. He just didn't want to see his friend get hurt.

The starting line was packed with dogs trying to get the best position. Kaltag, Nikki, and the other dogs were more than surprised when Balto trotted up.

"Balto! What are you, nuts? Steele catches you around here, he's going to turn you into kibble!" Kaltag warned.

"Let the half-dog run. It will be fun making him eat our snow," Nikki jeered.

But Balto just ignored them and focused on the course. His heart raced as he waited for the starting pistol. . . . *Bang!* At last—the dogs were off!

As the pack sped past, Jenna spotted a familiar gray blur. "Balto?" she gasped. Then, in a flash, the shape was gone.

Balto felt calm as his paws hit the ground in a easy rhythm—down the length of Front Street toward Snake

River. As the dogs headed south toward the shore, Balto easily passed the bulk of the pack, until there were just two dogs left in front of him. Then, as they looped back around Front Street toward the finish line, Balto zipped by another dog. Only Nikki was in front of him now.

Balto leaned into his stride. Nikki was tiring, Balto could tell. All he needed was one good burst of speed . . . and there it was! The next second, Balto streaked across the finish line, leaving Nikki in a spray of snow.

Balto had won! He was the fastest dog!

The racers gathered around the finish line. Balto panted with triumph as Jenna trotted up from across the street.

Suddenly Steele came from out of nowhere and started barking orders. "Okay, Nikki, Kaltag, Star, move it. We're strapping up!"

"Hey! Just a second there, Steele!" Balto protested. "I was the fastest dog!"

"You were the fastest *what?*" Steele asked cruelly. "Do you honestly think any musher would ever put you on his team? You're even more mixed-up than I thought!"

Then Jenna spoke up. "Steele, it doesn't matter who's on the team, as long as the medicine gets through. Stop being such a glory hound!"

"You're one hundred percent right, Jenna! I wasn't

thinking about those children. The important thing here is to get that medicine through. And that's just what I'm going to do." Steele's expression turned darker. He leaned in until he was nose-to-nose with Balto. "And when I come back, I'm going to fold you five ways and leave you for a cat toy," he hissed.

Just then the musher walked up, and instantly Steele turned into a big puppy.

"Good boy, Steele," said the musher. "Now let's take a look at our winner here." As the man bent down to inspect Balto, Steele stepped on Balto's paw. "YELP!" Balto cried out in pain.

The musher jumped back and stroked his beard. Then finally he spoke. "Well, we can't trust this one. He's part wolf. He might turn on me." He looked Balto over a second longer, then shook his head. His mind was made up. "Nikki, Kaltag, Star, let's go."

Steele grinned evilly at Balto before following his musher away. Balto just sat there, too stunned to move.

Jenna tried to comfort him. "Balto, I'm sor—"

"Better not talk to me, Jenna," Balto interrupted. "I might turn on you." Then he sprang to his feet and sped away.

"Balto, wait!" Jenna called. But Balto was gone.

▼▼▼

By evening, the new sled team was ready to go.

"Godspeed!"

"Good luck!"

Anxious villagers called out their farewells. From inside the hospital, Rosy and her parents watched the sled pull away. And just outside of town, on a lonely mound of snow, Balto sadly watched the sled race off into the night.

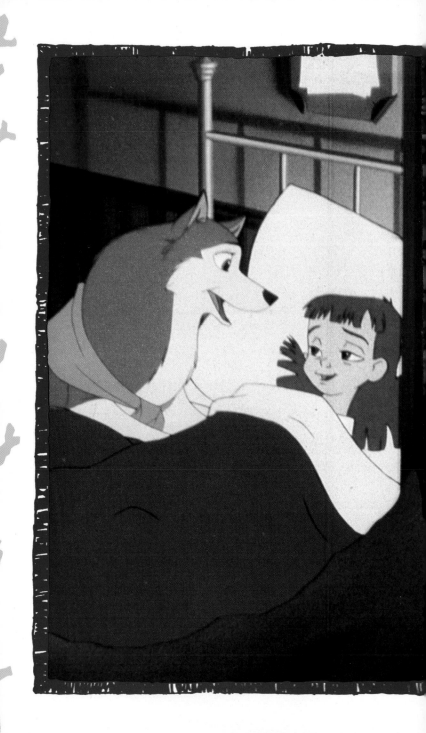

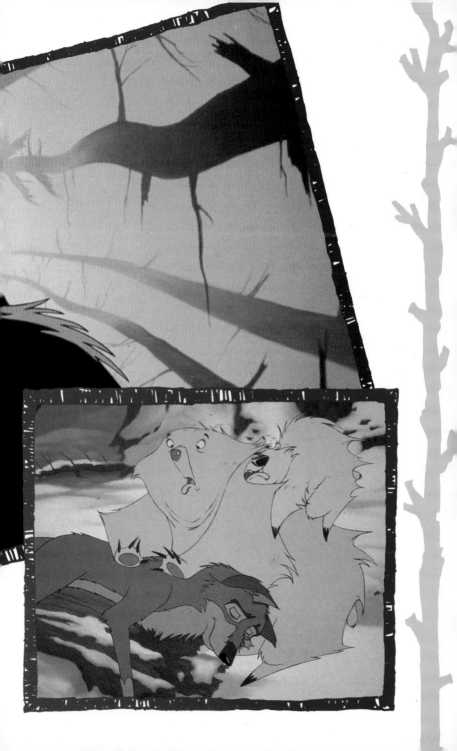

CHAPTER 5

The journey to Nenana was a smooth one. The team made fine time and the weather was good. *At this rate,* Steele thought, *we'll be home, planning my hero's parade, in no time.*

But by the time they left Nenana with their crate of antitoxin, a storm was brewing.

Tens of miles later, the storm was even worse. The snow was coming down so hard, the musher could barely see the team, let alone the trail. He just hoped Steele knew the way home and could pull them in the right direction.

Soon ice coated everything—the musher, the sled, even the dogs. Steele strained to see ahead in the wind-whipped snowy air. But it was useless. He stopped, panting hard, and looked around uncertainly, while the rest of the dogs waited nervously for Steele to tell them where to go.

"Steele!" Star yelled finally, struggling to be heard above the howling winds. "Maybe we should go back! We're lost."

"I am not lost!" Steele shouted.

"Lost? Did I say lost?" Star stammered. "You didn't let me finish . . . see, what I wanted to say . . . "

Steele cut him off. "It's . . . this way!"

Hours later, back in Nome, the silence of the sleeping town was shattered by a series of barks. A message had just come over the line, and Morse, the telegraph operator's dog, was rushing to get it out.

At the gold dredger, the dogs were assembled, waiting for the team's return. At the sound of Morse's barks, every ear pricked up and turned toward Doc, a wise Saint Bernard, for the translation of the code. At the end of the message, Doc sighed sadly and shook his head. "It's terrible, my friends, just terrible. Steele and his team are lost."

"When?"

"What happened?"

"What do you mean, lost?"

"They've missed their second checkpoint," Doc hurried to explain. "They're off the trail!"

The other dogs lowered their heads, too saddened by the news to speak. Finally a mutt named Wild Joe spoke up. "Can't they send another team?"

"It's too dangerous for us and our men," Doc replied.

"But . . . what about the little ones?" Another dog

named Chester voiced the question everyone was thinking.

Doc looked around the cabin slowly. "The medicine won't be here in time. We're going to lose them," he said sadly.

Balto overheard the whole thing from outside. "Rosy," he whispered.

Balto ran to the hospital. He peeked into Rosy's window and saw her father pleading with the doctor. "Please, Doctor. It's the only medicine we've got. Seeing Jenna might cheer her up."

The doctor nodded wearily, and Balto watched as Rosy's mother led Jenna into the room.

Jenna walked slowly to the little girl's bed. Rosy coughed and opened her eyes. "Jenna?" she asked in a weak voice.

Jenna nuzzled Rosy's hand with her nose. Rosy smiled, but her eyes soon fluttered closed again. Jenna and the adults could not hide their worried looks.

"Rosy," Balto whispered again from outside. He knew he had to do something. He couldn't just watch Rosy and the other children get sicker and sicker. He had to help—and he knew how. His mind made up, Balto raced toward home.

A little while later, Balto headed back into town—with Boris in tow.

"Balto, please! Don't go crazy on me now! Is foolishness!" Boris begged. "You will be frozen stiff by morning. When you are big frozen statue named Balto, don't come running to me."

But Balto wasn't listening. He walked with a purpose, and, as usual, Boris struggled to follow. Before long, Muk and Luk caught up with them, too. Luk made some questioning noises, and Muk started to translate, "He says . . . "

"'Where is Balto going?'" Boris interrupted. "He's going into freezing coldness to find dog he does not like, to bring medicine to town that does not like him!" Then Boris slapped himself on the head. "Oh, no! I am beginning to understand the bear!"

"Ooh," cooed Luk, his eyes wide with excitement. He nodded frantically.

"Yes! Yes! Count us in, too!" Muk shouted.

"Bears! Dogs!" Boris mumbled, disgusted.

Then Balto gently picked Boris up and set him down in front of the hospital window. Balto propped his own paws up on the sill, and they all peered into the dimly lit window. Inside the room, every bed was full—most with children.

Boris turned away. He didn't want to see any more. But he could feel Balto staring at him. Finally, he turned and looked into the next window. There was Rosy, lying very still. He could tell she was very sick. Boris hung his head. How could he not try to help

them? He took a deep breath. "So, we go get medicine," he announced.

"Wait a minute. Now you're coming?" Balto smiled at his friend.

Boris nodded. "Spending days in bitter cold, facing wild animals, risking death from exposure. Is like holiday in old country. Let's go."

Later that evening, Jenna watched Rosy sleeping from the bench outside the hospital. Exhausted herself, she rested her head on the windowsill a moment, then jerked her head up. What was that familiar smell? She sniffed the sill again.

Looking down, she saw several sets of prints she hadn't noticed before, leading out of town. Some looked like little bear paws, and one looked like a bird's, but one was made by very large paws—paws that only one dog could have made. "Balto!" Jenna exclaimed.

Slash! Balto's big paw slashed the tree trunk, leaving a distinctive mark.

"Good, Balto! You took on roughest, toughest, meanest tree in forest, and you won!" Boris said sarcastically.

"I'm marking the trail," Balto explained seriously.

He studied the marked tree carefully. *That should do it*, he thought. It would be easy to follow a trail of marked trees home.

"And here I am dropping bread crumbs!" Boris grunted.

Meanwhile, in another part of Alaska, the snow was raging around Steele and his team.

"Steele! We're going in circles!" Star shouted.

"What?" Steele barked in a threatening voice.

"Uh . . . circles is a good thing! I mean, they're . . . circular," Star struggled to finish.

"I know what I'm doing!" Steele said. But deep down, he wasn't so certain. *Which way?* Steele thought frantically. *Which way?* He would never admit he was lost—but which way? Panting hard, Steele looked to the left and to the right—then left and right again. "Come on!" he shouted.

Steele jerked the team left, but he still wasn't sure. He looked right again, this time only for a moment. But it was a moment too long. Steele hadn't noticed what was straight ahead of them—a steep ice slope! Frantically, he tried to turn back. But the team had already started pulling and it was too late to stop!

"Whoa! Whoa, Steele!" the musher shouted desperately as the team, sled, and musher slid across the ice. One after another, the dogs tumbled down the

slope, each going in a different direction as the sled whipped around wildly, bouncing off trees, rocks, and dogs. It shot through a thicket of trees—then suddenly ground to a jolting halt.

The musher collapsed onto the snow, still harnessed to the sled. He moaned just once, then lost consciousness. As the battered team worked to untangle themselves, Steele walked back to examine the musher.

"Looks like he's hurt bad, Steele," said one of the dogs.

"What are we going to do now?" Star asked.

Every dog on the team turned to Steele.

Steele didn't answer. He nudged the musher with his nose. The man didn't move. What *were* they going to do? They were hopelessly lost, with no musher to drive them. For the first time in his life, Steele was afraid.

CHAPTER 6

The sun shone down weakly on the tired search party. While Balto examined tracks in the snow, Muk and Luk amused themselves with a snowball war. Boris, of course, was not amused.

"Shhh!" he told them. "Balto is thinking." Then— *Smack!* A snowball exploded in his face.

"Brilliant, right on the beak!" Muk laughed. "What a bull's-eye!"

"Who did that?" Boris fluffed up his feathers and glared at the cubs.

"It was him!" Muk insisted.

Balto looked up and laughed as the cubs innocently pointed to each other. But he had more important things on his mind. He turned back to the trail, then over to a clump of trees. Was something moving in there?

Balto lifted his nose into the wind and sniffed. There was a strange smell in the air. He didn't know what it was, but it made him uneasy. "I think we should keep moving," Balto finally stated. "Muk, Luk, come on. Let's get going!"

"Is that your answer to all problems? Motion?" Boris complained. As Muk and Luk took off after Balto, Boris shook his head and hung back reluctantly. "'Come on Boris. Let's go, Boris. Faster, Boris,'" he grumbled. "Easy to say for a guy with four legs!"

Suddenly Boris was showered with snow. That was it! He spread his wings and called out dramatically, "Okay! Is time for goose to kick a little bear butt!"

Muk and Luk turned to look at him, and their mouths fell open. Boris watched as they grabbed each other, their eyes wide with fear.

"Ha! Finally your old Uncle Boris is making impression," Boris scoffed. Then something told him that Muk and Luk were not looking at him. . . .

Roar! Boris turned just in time to see a paw with razor-sharp claws whiz by him. The next second he was looking up into the huge fangs of a giant grizzly bear.

Boris flapped his wings and took off—only he was too panicked to look where he was going. *Smack!* Boris slammed into a tree.

A few yards ahead, Balto heard the grizzly's roar. Instantly, he raced back to Boris's defense. *Slash!* The grizzly swiped at Boris again. He missed, but hit the tree hard enough to send the whole thing flying. It landed squarely on Muk and Luk, pinning them in place.

Balto dove for the grizzly, but was easily knocked away. Boris and the cubs, too scared and stunned to move, just stared as the grizzly's shadow loomed over them. Then Balto was there again—chomping down hard on the grizzly's leg. Furious, the bear slashed at Balto. But Balto held on tight and brought the grizzly crashing to all fours.

Somehow the grizzly shook himself loose. He swiped at Balto and clipped him, and Balto felt himself flying through the air and into a tree. He slid down the trunk, dazed. He struggled to get up, but he couldn't get his bearings. Before him, the grizzly reared up on his hind legs, preparing for a final attack. Boris and the cubs watched helplessly, petrified with fear.

ROAR!

Suddenly something streaked between Balto and the grizzly. Balto shook his head, and when his vision finally cleared, he smiled weakly. *Jenna!*

With one great leap, Jenna landed squarely on the grizzly's shoulder and sank her teeth deep into his joint. Enraged, the bear swiped at Jenna, clawing her leg. Jenna dropped from the grizzly, gasping in pain.

While Jenna sprawled there with the wind knocked out of her, the bear turned his attention back to Balto. But Balto's strength had returned. He lunged at the grizzly and landed on his back. Then he clamped his jaws tightly down on the bear's neck.

Stunned and in pain, the bear lost his balance and tumbled down a snowbank and onto a sheet of ice—dragging Balto with him.

Then Jenna, Boris, and the cubs heard an explosive sound. . . . *C-R-R-A-A-C-K!* Balto's friends raced to the edge of the hill just in time to see the frozen river crack and split beneath the bear's enormous weight.

"Balto!" Jenna and Boris shouted at the same time. Suddenly the gap widened, and the grizzly plunged into the freezing water—followed by Balto!

Boris and Jenna looked on in shock as the churning current swept the grizzly away. But where was Balto?

"Geronimo!" Muk and Luk raced down the snowbank. Fearlessly, they dove into the icy river after Balto.

"Luk! Muk!" Jenna called. The cubs were nowhere to be seen.

"They cannot swim!" Boris cried.

"What! Polar bears who can't swim?" Jenna said. Then suddenly she spotted Balto. He was trapped underneath a layer of ice.

"He's drowning! NO!" Jenna shouted frantically as the ice carried Balto farther and farther away.

Boris searched for a sign of the cubs. He stuck his head under the ice, then straightened up, shaking his head, with a scared look on his face. "I don't see them."

"Where are they?" Jenna asked desperately.

Crash! Suddenly Luk burst through the ice. In seconds, Muk followed, coughing and holding on to Balto.

"*Balto!*" Jenna shouted. "Muk! Luk!" She waited anxiously with Boris as the cubs dragged a semiconscious Balto to shore. They all gathered around Balto, who was lying very still.

"Balto, are you okay? Say something!" Muk shouted.

"Come to life, come to life! Breathe! Come on—breathe!" Boris pleaded.

"Is he going to be okay? Is he going to be okay? Uncle Boris, tell us he's going to be okay!" Muk pleaded. "Because he doesn't look very well, does he?"

Finally Balto began to stir. He coughed up water, then opened his eyes and slowly focused on his friends.

Boris let out a deep sigh of relief. "Balto! I was so scared, I got people bumps!"

Balto smiled at his friend warmly. "Boris, I know you think this trip is crazy," he said, "but I'm glad you came."

"Who else should you bring on a wild goose chase but a goose?" Boris joked.

Then Balto saw Jenna.

"Are you okay?" they both asked at the same time, then laughed.

"I'm fine," Jenna answered, smiling. Then her face grew serious. "Look, a message came through town. We have to take the mountain trail."

"But if we take Eagle Pass, it'll save half a day!" Balto said. He started to stand.

Jenna shook her head and explained. "It's blocked. The mountain trail is dangerous, but we can do it."

"I'm beginning to see there isn't anything you can't do," Balto said, impressed.

"I am seeing a few things, too," Boris mumbled as he watched the two dogs stare into each other's eyes. "Is making the ice melt."

Unaware of the romantic moment, Muk and Luk shook themselves dry, showering Boris with a fine spray of ice.

"I hate bears!" Boris grumbled. But he was smiling.

Balto laughed. "You guys ought to learn how to swim someday. You'd be very good at it."

The cubs looked at each other for a moment, then grinned proudly. Luk began to make swimming motions with his arms.

"Well, of course we were!" Muk shouted. "We were in the water. We were moving, we got wet! We . . . *Luk*, we were *swimming!*" He threw his arms in the air. Everyone laughed.

Then Jenna tried to stand up. But she quickly stumbled. "Oh, clumsy," she explained. But Balto could see she was in pain. He looked down at the

deep gash the bear had left in her leg.

"You're hurt," Balto said.

"I'm fine," Jenna said confidently. She took a few steps to prove it and stumbled again. "Ow! Maybe I'm not so fine," she said slowly. She sighed. "You should all go ahead without me."

"Jenna—" Balto began.

"No." Jenna stopped him. "No. I'd be slowing everyone down. And Rosy can't hold out much longer."

Balto could see Jenna's mind was made up. He dragged a large fir branch over to her. "Muk, you and Luk carry Jenna back to town on this," Balto instructed.

"And this time, no time out for a swim," Boris teased.

"You can make sure of that, Boris," Balto said. "*You* have to lead them home. Just follow my marks."

"You're going on . . . alone?" Jenna asked.

"It won't be the first time," Balto said.

Jenna nodded. She slipped her bandanna off her neck and placed it around Balto's. "Here. I'm afraid it won't keep you very warm," she said, nudging it into place.

"Yes, it will," Balto assured her.

As they got ready to leave, Luk made several worried sounds.

"Well, of course Balto'll come back," Muk

replied. "He's Balto, isn't he?" They both looked at Balto.

"I'm coming back with the medicine. I promise," Balto said firmly. Then in a cheerful voice, he went on, "Go ahead, guys, get Jenna home."

As Luk and Muk helped Jenna onto the branch "sled," Boris hung back with Balto. "I do not like leaving you out here alone, Balto," he said. "Who is going to tell you how cold you are?"

Balto looked Boris right in the eye. "Boris, they need you even more than I do."

Boris nodded. He knew his friend was right. "Let me tell you something, Balto," he said. "A dog cannot make this journey alone. But . . . maybe a wolf can!"

With that, Boris turned to the cubs and took charge. "Right! You two balls of fluff! Let's move!" he shouted. "Honk, two, three, four. Honk, two, three, four."

Balto watched his friends move away from him, then turned in the opposite direction and disappeared into the snowy mist.

At that very moment, a telegraph message was coming into Nome:

NOME. STOP.
CANNOT SEND MORE ANTITOXIN. STOP.

WEATHER TOO SEVERE. STOP.
LOST SLED TEAM ONLY HOPE. STOP.
OUR PRAYERS ARE WITH THEM. STOP.
ANCHORAGE. STOP

CHAPTER 7

As the sun sank over the horizon, Balto forged on alone into the worsening storm, stopping now and then to sniff and mark a tree. By the time darkness fell, Balto was exhausted. *I should've found them by now,* he thought.

Then at the top of the next hill, Balto smelled something familiar. He looked down into the valley. Slowly, the moon moved out from behind some clouds . . . and there they were! Steele, the overturned sled, and the other dogs!

While the dogs huddled for warmth near the unconscious musher, Steele paced anxiously. No one even noticed Balto until he was practically beside them.

"Balto?" Star said in disbelief.

"Balto! How did you find us?"

Balto looked from dog to dog. "Is anyone hurt?" he asked.

Steele stepped up before they could respond. "Everyone is fine," he growled. He moved between

Balto and the sled, his lips curled into a snarl.

"Yeah, but our musher hit his head. He didn't get up," Star tried to explain.

"And he's not moving," Nikki added.

"All right. Follow me. I can lead you home," Balto told them.

But Steele had other ideas. "We don't need your help," he snapped.

"Maybe we should listen to Balto," Star begged.

Steele swung around to glare at Star and growled. Star cringed and shut his mouth.

"Well . . . how would youse get us home, dere?" Nikki asked Balto.

"I marked the trail. Like this." Balto swiped a tree. The dogs were clearly impressed. And that made Steele even more furious.

"*I'll* get us back," barked Steele. "*I'm* the lead dog! *I'm* in charge!" He moved up as if to chase Balto away.

But Balto wasn't backing down. "Then let me just take back the medicine," he begged. "The children are getting sicker." He looked at the sled and the box of antitoxin.

Steele was panting now. "You touch that box and I'll tear you apart!"

"Steele! I'm not leaving without that medicine," Balto said flatly, holding his ground.

"Who do you think you are?" Steele snarled.

"Since when do you need a pedigree to help someone?" replied Balto. "Let me help you." Balto walked past Steele deliberately, and with an angry roar, Steele charged Balto and knocked him down.

Balto rose, shaking off the snow. "I don't want to fight," he said. And once again he started toward the medicine. But Steele was determined to keep Balto away. He attacked again—this time going for Balto's throat—as the other dogs watched helplessly. They would have followed Balto in an instant, but they had never crossed Steele before—and they weren't about to start now.

Steele and Balto tumbled in the snow. Balto struggled to get to the crate. But this time Steele had a grip on Jenna's bandanna. He swung and threw Balto against a snowbank.

With a loud thud, Balto's head hit a hard patch of ice. He lay very still, his eyes closed. Jenna's bandanna fell to the snow beside him.

Steele laughed victoriously. But before he knew it, Balto was up again. With a fiery glow in his eyes, Balto moved forward, edging Steele back toward a steep ravine. Steele tried to hold his ground, but Balto caught him completely off guard. Suddenly Balto lunged forward, and Steele leaped back—into thin air! With one last yelp, Steele plunged out of sight.

Panting, Balto looked back at the team, ready for

anyone else who would challenge him. But the team was too shocked. They had never seen anyone beat Steele before. As Balto watched, they lined up respectfully by their harnesses. Then Star nudged the lead harness in Balto's direction.

The lead dog! Finally, Balto was leading a team!

Balto made sure the musher and the antitoxin were secure on the sled. Then he took his position at the head of the line. He looked back at his team, nodded approvingly, and began to pull. "*Mush!*" he shouted.

Minutes later, as the sled headed off toward Nome, Steele slowly climbed his way back up the ravine. "Go ahead, wolf dog!" he hissed. "You'll never get home. I'll make sure of that!" Then he picked up Jenna's bandanna and ran out of the valley.

Steele lumbered alone through the forest, back toward Nome. Blinded by hate and the need for revenge, he was looking for one thing—and one thing only.

Aha! He saw it. A slash across the trunk of a tree. Steele raised his paw and slashed across the mark, making it impossible to see. Then he darted to another tree—and another—and another—until he had made a circle of identically marked trees.

No way was he going to let that half-breed mutt,

Balto, get all the glory. If Steele couldn't bring the medicine back, no one would.

Later, Balto found one of the first marked trees and smiled. They were on the right track. Even in the murky darkness, he knew he was going the right way.

But then Balto noticed the tree next to it. It was marked, too. And the one next to that. And the one next to that. In fact, they were surrounded by identically marked trees.

Balto slowed, then stopped. *It's not possible!* he thought. Then he sniffed the tree. There was another dog's scent on it—and that dog was Steele!

Balto looked around, growing more and more worried. His scent—his trail—were completely gone!

"Which way, Balto? Which way?" Star asked.

Balto looked around desperately. "Uh, this way," he mumbled.

As he led the sled through the forest, Balto realized with horror just how much damage Steele had done. Balto's trail had been completely destroyed. Now he was as lost as Steele had been.

Hours later, Balto passed the same gnarled tree for the second, or maybe even third, time. Panting, Balto shook his head. "No, it can't be!"

"Balto, why are you taking us in circles?" Kaltag barked.

"I'm not! I mean . . . I don't know!" Balto gestured toward the marked trees surrounding them. "It's Steele!"

"Maybe we was better off with Steele," Nikki muttered.

"No! Come on! *Mush!*" Balto yelled. He ran wildly, while the rest of the team tried to keep up. As they raced toward a cluster of trees, the antitoxin skidded dangerously across the sled.

"Balto! Slow down! Please!" Star begged.

But Balto kept going, through a cluster of marked trees—and straight toward the edge of a cliff!

Balto tried desperately to stop the sled, but it was too late! The sled flipped onto its side, throwing the unconscious musher into the snow, and sliding closer and closer to the cliff's jagged edge.

The crate of antitoxin rocked this way and that as the sled bounced along. At last it broke from its ropes and flew through the air—toward the cliff!

Balto lunged for it—catching the straps of the crate in his teeth at the very last minute, just as the sled skidded to a stop, barely a foot from the cliff's edge. The group let loose a collective sigh of relief . . . then they heard a deafening noise. ROAR! The cliff was false, made only of ice and snow. Bit by bit, it crumbled away under Balto's paws!

Balto scrambled for solid ground—but the next

thing he knew, he and the crate were headed straight down.

Meanwhile, back in Nome, Jenna had returned to the gold dredger. While Doc cleaned her bear wounds, the other dogs looked on with concern.

"I don't get it," Wild Joe said. "How could Balto hope to find Steele and his team? They were off the trail."

"Well . . . he's tracking them," Jenna explained.

"That mutt? Tracking a championship team in a blizzard?" Morse laughed, and some of the other dogs joined in. They stopped abruptly when the door slammed open, letting in a gust of icy wind and . . . *Steele!*

Jenna looked up. "Balto?" she cried hopefully. Then she saw who it was.

"Steele!"

"You're back!"

"We'd given you up!"

The dogs ushered Steele into the warm cabin and offered him a bone.

"Where are the others?" asked Doc.

Steele bowed his head and began his act. "One by one they fell," Steele said slowly. "Frozen, barely alive. I pulled four onto the sled and three more on my back. I walked and walked, but it was too late. They

were . . . " He paused dramatically, shaking his head and playing up to his audience.

The other dogs gasped.

"What about the medicine?" Doc asked.

Steele continued, "I went on, dragging the medicine alone. Suddenly that wolf dog appeared. Balto demanded I let *him* take the medicine." Steele turned to Jenna. "You know he just wanted so much to be a hero in your eyes."

Then he turned back to the others. "He grabbed the crate, but he couldn't handle it. He didn't see the patch of ice . . . and the cliff. . . ." Steele pulled Jenna's now ragged bandanna out from under his collar and tossed it at her feet. "He didn't have a chance." He shook his head, clucking sadly.

"My bandanna!" Jenna gasped.

Steele slid closer to her. "He made me promise to take care of you, Jenna," he whispered.

"You're lying," Jenna cried with an angry look in her eye. "Balto's alive. And he's coming home." Then she picked up her bandanna and walked away.

CHAPTER
8

As the wind whipped the snow around him wildly, Balto struggled to climb out of the canyon he had fallen into. But the snow was too deep and the cliff was too steep. *I've let Jenna down,* he thought. *How could I have thought I could bring the team back by myself?*

Then suddenly something made Balto look up. Someone was watching him. A wolf—a white wolf. The wolf stared into Balto's eyes. "*Hoooowwwwwllllll!*" he called, and waited for Balto's response.

Balto had to turn away. He was ashamed to meet the great wolf's eyes. When he finally looked back, the white wolf was gone. Balto gazed around. That's when he saw the corner of the antitoxin crate peeking out of the snow. For an instant, Balto had hope. Then he looked up toward the top of the ravine. It was a long, long way up. Could he make it?

Then Balto remembered Boris's last words to him: "*Let me tell you something, Balto. A dog cannot make this*

journey alone. But maybe a wolf can." Taking a deep breath, Balto searched for a way to begin the climb. He sniffed the ground and noticed the white wolf's tracks. Hesitantly, Balto placed one of his paws into one of the prints. It was a perfect fit!

Suddenly, the wolf appeared again. This time at the top of the ravine. He howled again encouragingly to Balto. And this time Balto howled back.

At the top of the cliff, the rest of the team stood around nervously. Then they too heard the howls.

"Oh, great! As if things were not bad enough, now we got wolves," Nikki groaned.

"Wolves!" the other dogs exclaimed, alarmed.

"Hey! Over here!" Kaltag called, looking over the edge of the cliff.

The team peered over the side just in time to see Balto climbing up the slope, dragging the antitoxin crate with his teeth.

"Balto?" Star called.

"And he's got the medicine! Come on! You can make it!" Nikki barked. "Hey, he has got the feet of a wolf, dere," he said with admiration.

The dogs barked their encouragement to Balto. As he reached the edge of the cliff, they gathered to help pull the crate up and load it back onto the sled.

"Let's go home!" Balto said, panting, when they were done. Immediately the dogs lined up and slipped into position. And once again, Star respect-

fully offered up the lead dog's harnesses and Balto took his place at the head of the team.

"*Mush!*" Balto commanded.

With new energy, the team entered the forest of randomly marked trees. But instead of looking at the trees, Balto sniffed the air and the ground to find the trail. This time Balto's instincts would lead him home. He only hoped they weren't too late!

Boris, Muk, and Luk were snuggled close together in the old trawler when they heard the sound of bells and the howl of a wolf off in the distance. It sounded like . . .

"Balto?" Boris exclaimed. "Balto's *back!*"

In an instant, they were rushing toward the sound.

All over Nome, people were rising, peering out of their windows, and rushing out into the street. They clapped and cheered as Balto proudly led his team down Front Street.

Inside the gold dredger, Steele was still telling his story. " . . . I swam and swam. It was freezing cold. Then finally, I said to myself, 'Steele, you just have to gnaw your way to the surface. . . . '"

Suddenly every ear perked up at the sound of bells and howls. "It's Balto, with the medicine!" Doc shouted. He dashed outside, followed by the other dogs.

"I can explain," Steele called after them. "See . . . uh, you guys weren't there so you don't . . . wait . . . guys, wait just a second, please?" But by then, Steele was all alone.

In town, the sled team continued until they reached the hospital steps. As the orderlies rushed out to collect the medicine and the unconscious musher, the jubilant crowd surrounded Balto.

Embarrassed, Balto shrugged off the lead harnesses as hands that had once tried to keep him away now reached out to embrace him. He was glad when Boris finally ran up and threw his wings around him.

"Not dog! Not wolf!" Boris shouted. "You are hero!"

Then Rosy's father came out of the hospital. "Come on, boy," he called to Balto. "There's someone who wants to see you."

Balto smiled and bashfully followed the man into Rosy's room. The doctor had just given her the antitoxin shot.

In a minute, Rosy's eyes fluttered open. "Mommy?" she called.

"Rosy, darling!" Rosy's mother cried.

"I fell asleep," Rosy said.

"Oh, Rosy!" Rosy's father reached down to hold her.

Just then, Balto noticed Rosy's musher's hat, forgotten on the floor. He picked it up and walked slowly to her bed.

Rosy looked down and smiled. "Balto! I'd be lost without you!" she said as she took the musher's cap and put it on.

Balto beamed, and Rosy's father gently patted his head. Then Balto sensed someone else looking at him. He turned toward the doorway and smiled. It was Jenna.

Balto and Jenna nuzzled each other, happy to be together again. Then, as they listened to the cheers coming from the street, Jenna gave Balto a little nudge. It was time to greet his fans.

A few moments later, Balto humbly emerged onto Front Street and a rousing cheer rang through the air. "Balto! Balto! Balto the hero!!!"

And do you know, it hasn't stopped yet!